E R

Russo, Marisabina

Grandpa Abe

$14.93

W9-BMU-779

BAKER & TAYLOR

GRANDPA ABE

by Marisabina Russo

Greenwillow Books · New York

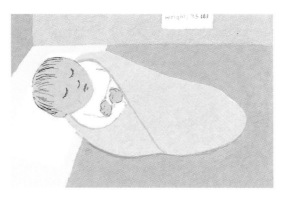

When I was born, my grandma came to see me in the hospital with her boyfriend, Abe. She snuck him into the room by telling the nurse he was my grandfather. Mama got mad at Grandma.

"Abe is not Sarah's grandfather!" said Mama. "You only met him last month!"

"Every baby needs a grandpa," said Grandma.

When I was christened, Abe came to my party. Mama let him hold me.

Abe held me up against his sweater. "I've never held such a tiny baby," he said.

Then I spit up on his shoulder.

Abe just laughed and laughed.

On my first birthday, I started to cry when everyone sang "Happy Birthday."

"Don't cry, little pumpkin," said Grandma. "I have good news for you. Abe and I are getting married. You're going to have a grandpa!"

When I was two, Abe gave me a soft white teddy bear
with a black nose. And a book. And a puzzle.

"You are spoiling her," said Mama.

"I have to spoil Sarah," said Abe. "She's my only
grandchild."

When I was three, my favorite food was spaghetti. So was Abe's. We both ate it with sauce. We both got sauce on our chins and sometimes on our shirts.

Mama, Grandma, and Daddy couldn't believe how much we ate.

"Sarah, you sure take after your grandpa," said Grandma.

When I was four, Abe kept finding candy behind my
right ear.
"Whoops, there's another one," he'd say, catching
a peppermint candy and giving it to me.
I tried and tried, but I only felt my hair behind my ear.

When I was five, Mama played music. Grandma and Abe danced around the living room.

"Your turn, Sarah," said Abe, taking my arm. He spun me around and around.

When the music stopped, I felt dizzy and silly. Abe was out of breath.

When I was six, Abe drew me a picture of a circus clown.
And an elephant. And a juggler. Then he drew a picture
of me in a ballerina's tutu.
I hung all the pictures on the wall next to my bed.

When I was seven, Abe did magic tricks for all my friends. He made cards disappear and eggs roll out of his sleeve.

Everybody ooohed and ahhhed.

Then Abe taught us his magic thumb trick. We could all do it by the end of the party.

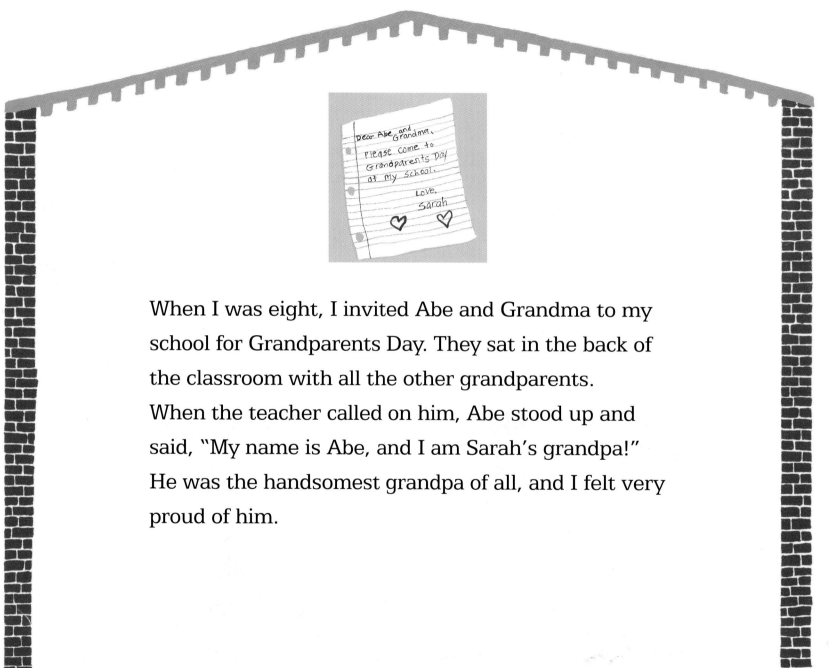

When I was eight, I invited Abe and Grandma to my school for Grandparents Day. They sat in the back of the classroom with all the other grandparents.

When the teacher called on him, Abe stood up and said, "My name is Abe, and I am Sarah's grandpa!" He was the handsomest grandpa of all, and I felt very proud of him.

When I was nine, something terrible happened.

One morning Abe died. Grandma called us.

Mama cried. Daddy hugged Mama.

I didn't believe it. Not at all.

We went to Grandma's apartment.

Abe's glasses were on the night table. Abe's comb was in the bathroom. The wooden box for pencils that I had painted for him for Christmas was sitting on his desk.

Mama got a shopping bag and filled it with Abe's things.

"What are you doing?" I asked.

"It makes Grandma too sad," said Mama.

"But that stuff all belongs to Grandpa Abe!" I said.

"Sarah, Grandpa Abe is dead," said Mama.

We stayed with Grandma that night and the next.

I slept in Grandma's bed right next to her. Usually

Grandma snores, but I didn't hear any snoring.

At the funeral Grandma cried and cried. She squeezed

my hand.

I didn't cry. I couldn't believe my grandpa Abe was dead.

Later at Grandma's I sat on her bed while Grandma changed into her slippers.

The closet door was open. I could see Abe's sweaters neatly stacked on a shelf.

"May I have one of Grandpa Abe's sweaters?" I asked.

"Of course, darling," said Grandma.

I pulled out a blue sweater. It smelled like Abe. I put it on. It reached my knees.

"I'm going to keep this forever," I said.

Grandma took my hand. "Let's go have some cake and milk," she said.

We walked into the kitchen. Everyone was sitting
around the table talking about Abe.
I did Abe's magic thumb trick.
Grandma smiled and kissed me on the cheek.

For Stephen Kalich

Gouache paints were used for the full-color art. The text type is Egyptian 505 Roman.
Printed in Hong Kong by South China Printing Company (1988) Ltd.   First Edition 10 9 8 7 6 5 4 3 2 1

Library of Congress Cataloging-in-Publication Data
Russo, Marisabina.
Grandpa Abe / by Marisabina Russo.
p.   cm.
Summary: Grandpa Abe enters Sarah's life as her grandmother's boyfriend,
becomes her grandfather by marriage, and enriches her life before leaving it.
ISBN 0-688-14097-1 (trade).   ISBN 0-688-14098-X (lib. bdg.)
[1. Grandfathers—Fiction.   2. Death—Fiction.]   I. Title.
PZ7.R9192Gr   1996   [E]—dc20
95-2260   CIP   AC